This book belongs to:

_____

_____

_____

For Mum and Dad, who made sure that
Father Christmas always found me

J. R.

For the amazing Barney, Joshua, John and
Lydia with thanks for being you

T. B.

Fletcher and the Snowflake Christmas.
Published in Great Britain 2020 by
Graffeg Limited.

Written by Julia Rawlinson copyright © 2010.
Illustrated by Tiphanie Beeke copyright © 2010.
Designed and produced by Graffeg Limited
copyright © 2020.

First published in Great Britain in 2010
by Gullane Children's Books.

Graffeg Limited, 24 Stradey Park Business
Centre, Mwrwg Road, Llangennech, Llanelli,
Carmarthenshire SA14 8YP Wales UK.
Tel 01554 824000. www.graffeg.com.

Julia Rawlinson is hereby identified as the author
of this work in accordance with section 77 of the
Copyrights, Designs and Patents Act 1988.

A CIP Catalogue record for this book is
available from the British Library.

ISBN 9781913134655

1 2 3 4 5 6 7 8 9

Fletcher and the Snowflake Christmas

Julia Rawlinson & Tiphanie Beeke

GRAFFEG

It was an ice-bright Christmas Eve, and the sky was a dazzling blue. Every tree in the wood was frost-sprinkled and sparkling, and frozen puddles creaked and crackled under Fletcher's paws. He padded down the burrow-bank where the rabbits used to live, and bounced over the fallen tree that blocked their old front door.

And stopped. And looked.

And had a terrible thought…

How was Father Christmas going to find the
rabbits' new home?

Fletcher shivered as a chill wind sliced through the wood,
rattling the bare branches. He thought about how sad he
would feel if he had to leave his cosy den. He thought
about how the rabbits would feel if
Father Christmas did not come.
And then he thought about...

...arrows!

Fletcher began to scrunch around,
collecting sticks from the frosty
ground, making a trail of arrows,
leading to the new burrow.

"What are you doing?" asked Squirrel,
looking down from the branches.
"Making a trail to the rabbits' new burrow
for Father Christmas," said Fletcher.
"Otherwise they might not get their presents,"
gulped Squirrel, and he scampered down to
help Fletcher collect more sticks.

Soon a flock of birds had gathered in the
treetops, their feathers fluffed against the
cold, to see what was going on.

"We're making a trail to the rabbits' new burrow," said Fletcher.
"For Father Christmas," added Squirrel.
"We'll help you!" chirped the birds.

The trail passed between bare trees and crossed
the tinkling, ice-rimmed stream, as the sun began to
set, turning a dazzling gold. Fletcher and Squirrel
shivered with cold and hurried up the little
hill to where the mice were draping their nest
with holly and ivy leaves.
"What are you doing?" asked the mice.

"We're making a trail,"
said Fletcher.

"To the rabbits' new
burrow," added Squirrel.

"For Father Christmas,"
added the birds.
"You'd better hurry," said the
mice. "It's getting late.
We'll help you!"

So Fletcher, Squirrel, the birds and the mice finished the trail to the
rabbits' new home, which was sweet with the smell of blackberry pie,
cosy and warm. They gathered round the crackling fire, thawing out
their icy noses, nibbling pieces of pie and singing Christmas songs. And
while Squirrel put on a juggling show with holly berries and mistletoe,
outside in the shivery darkness…

...it began to snow.
Fat white flakes tumbled softly from a heavy sky.

They landed, light and whisper-quiet,
on the frozen ground.

And when Fletcher went to the burrow door to go
home for the night, the snow was soft and deep and white,
and all the arrows had gone.
"Oh no!" cried Fletcher, blinking back tears.
"What will happen to your presents now? Father Christmas
will never be able to find your home."
Fletcher stared out into the darkness, imagining
Father Christmas lost in the snow.

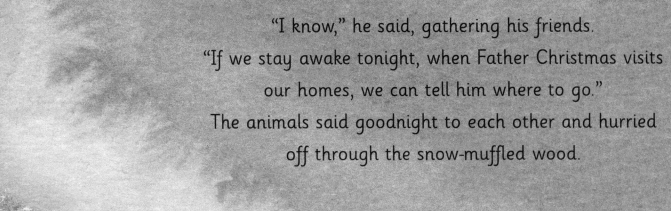

"I know," he said, gathering his friends.
"If we stay awake tonight, when Father Christmas visits
our homes, we can tell him where to go."
The animals said goodnight to each other and hurried
off through the snow-muffled wood.

Fletcher snuggled down in his warm,
soft bed to keep watch for Father Christmas.

But curled in the cosy
hollow of an oak tree,
Squirrel began to snore.

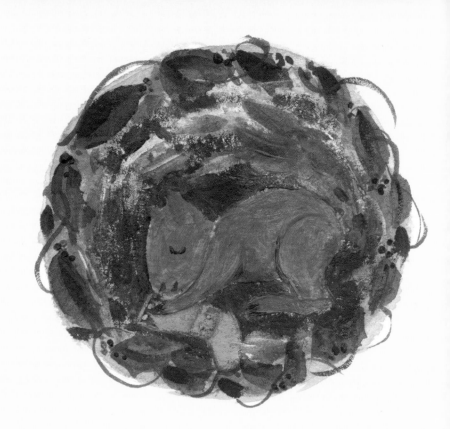

High in the snowy
branches of a fir tree, the
birds began to doze.

In their toasty warm
nest, the mice dreamt of
ribbon-wrapped berries.

And in his snug little bed,
Fletcher's eyes closed.

So when Father Christmas came
to call, everyone was fast asleep.
And next morning, when Fletcher
rushed to the rabbits' burrow...

...Father Christmas had found them after all!

"I'm sorry I went to sleep" puffed Fletcher,
"but I've brought you a Christmas rose."
"And we've brought nuts," panted Squirrel,
pulling the mice through the snow.
"And we've brought berries," sang the birds,
spiralling in the snow-bright sky.

"And best of all you've brought yourselves.
There's room in the burrow for everyone...

Happy Christmas!"

cried the rabbits, and they welcomed their friends into
the berry-bright warmth of their home.

Fletcher's Four Seasons

Discover the delight of the seasons in these exquisite and uplifting picture books.

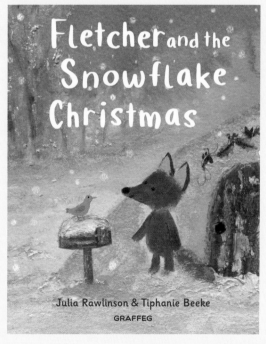